UNFOLDING

SHORT STORIES

VICTORIA HOPE

UNFOLDING

Copyright © 2020 Victoria Hope

This book is a work of fiction. Names, characters, businesses, organisations, places, events and incidents either are the product of the author's imagination or are used fictitiously. Any resemblance to actual persons, living or dead, events, or locales is entirely coincidental.

www.victoriahope.co.uk

Book and Cover design by Victoria Hope
Cover photo by Alice Donovan Rouse

ISBN: 9798605846215

First edition: 2020

Revised edition: 2021

10 9 8 7 6 5 4 3 2 1

For

Little Me

"Keep your heart open to dreams. For as long as
there's a dream, there is hope, and as long as there is
hope, there is joy in living."

Anon

CONTENTS

Author's Note

Unfolding is a collection of ten short stories, each with their own surprise. While some may thrill you, others will leave you with a smile. I hope with every turn of the page you'll uncover something new, a new character, a new experience, a new perspective. As I've grown and evolved, my stories too have evolved. For this reason they are arranged, for the most part, in the order in which they were written. On my journey I've discovered, as you will as well, how our words have the power to thrill, to excite, to shock, but ultimately to inspire, to uplift, to illuminate. Each story will unfold in its own unique way, but the book itself is a personal accomplishment, one which I hope you will read again and again as you too grow, learn, and evolve. This is the journey of life; this is the beauty of its *Unfolding*.

1

MIRROR, MIRROR

MY INSIDES SQUIRM AS I spot a young couple exchange saliva as I leave the park. *As bad as Kevin when he's got his hands all over that female of his.* Melissa, little blonde thing with the funny accent, s*outhern*. Thinks Kevin is the bee's knees. *Wait until she finds out he's the whole damn hornets' nest.*

Can't blame her though, really. Kevin has a way with the female species, *or so he tells me.* Honestly, with all that bullshit he talks it's no wonder they all worship him. Heck, even I'd fall for it if I didn't know what Kevin was really like. *If I couldn't see inside his head.*

Hot, thick java burns into my chest bringing me back to my surroundings.

'I'm sorry, so sorry!' A woman pants, attempting to dab me with her filthy napkin. One of those overly apologetic women, incapable of keeping even coffee in her cup. Chipped red nail polish and split ends tells me she doesn't take much pride in her appearance. Nevertheless, I pity her for her incompetence and for ruining my white shirt. I swipe her away, giving her a disgruntled look.

One, two, three, I count, taking the stairs to my apartment instead of the germ-infested elevator. If this was Kevin, he'd have taken the elevator, no matter how fit he is. That's the problem with Kevin, *he always cheats.*

I hope Mrs Duvall doesn't stop me again, *twenty-seven, twenty-eight*, I'm allergic to her scent. Not perfume but something far worse, even worse than wet dog, *poor hygiene.* I hear her filthy slippers flip-flop towards the inside of door 28 as I reach the third floor. I sneak past the spy hole before she spots me. *Thirty-six, thirty-seven.* I reach my door, turning the door handle gingerly with my handkerchief. Cool air welcomes me, and the sight of my home comforts invites me in. *A place for everything and everything in its place.* It's perfectly quiet in here, not a sound. *No Kevin.*

My watch reads seven-thirty-four, *another minute.* I wait, feet firmly planted on the kitchen tiles, s*even thirty-five. Click,* the coffee machine roars to life. One great thing about being a freelance writer, I can work from home. No idle chit-chat with the Jane Doe to my left, whom I have no interest in communicating with, nor do I find her incessant whining about her kids and her husband to be of any importance to me. No, none of that. Just me, myself and…Kevin, usually. Though nothing he ever says makes much sense either. Normally some nonsensical yak about the gym, he goes on and on as I sit back with clenched fists, watching as he makes a mess of my kitchen. I like to think of him as my brother from the wrong side of the tracks. He looks out for me; I clean up after him.

Mother didn't like Kevin, that's why we got our own place. Mother said we wouldn't make it on our own, 'Wouldn't amount to anything,' she said.

Mother doesn't phone anymore.

I stagger to her door, pounding my battered fists on the glossy finish. When that doesn't work, I try slamming the gold knocker until it leaves an indent in the door. No luck.

Thinks she can just blow me off like she has. Ignore my calls, make it look like I'm the clingy one? I guess she's still mad about the other night, not that I can remember a damn thing. Jason said he tried to stop me, said I got so mad I put my fist through his glass table! Thinking 'bout that now, Melissa did the right thing in running off. Jason said she'd gone; said he'd clean it up. I went to lie down for a while, don't like it when I can't remember stuff. Must of dozed off 'cos next thing I hear, Jason's tapping away on that computer of his. All through the night, all I hear is tap-tap-tap! Jason doesn't sleep much, I'm the opposite, I can sleep for days sometimes...

I give up trying the door, 'Well screw you then, princess!' I pound the buttons on the elevator until the doors open, 'piece of crap!'

The street's bustlin' with all kinds of faces, none I care to look at. *Bunch of jerks.*

'Hey! Watch where you're going!' some jackass slams past me on his way through the crowds. I make a grab for the back of his sweater but he's too far past me now. Blood pounds in my ears. I can practically hear that do-gooder Jason telling me to calm down.

I light a cigarette and prop myself up against a wall for a minute. If I wasn't directly opposite, if I hadn't of stopped where I was, I wouldn't have noticed it at all.

Smoke burns my lungs as I choke. A missing poster, *'Woman, 5ft 2, blonde hair, blue eyes...'* I would have walked straight past her, *Melissa.*

All kinds of things start running through my mind, making the blood pulsate in my head even louder. *Missing?* No, no she can't be. *She can't be!* I only saw her the other night, *or was it a week ago?* I don't remember. I'll ask Jason, he's the brains, he'll know. *If someone's hurt her, I'll...I'll kill them!*

Our dodgy elevator crawls up to the fourth floor. Any second now it will drop back down I'm sure of it! Unfortunately, it doesn't. My footing heavy as I enter the apartment. No sound of Jason, no sign of him at all. Computer's cold. My heart's beating so fast, even faster than he types!

Something crunches beneath my feet. There, embedded in the carpet. Holding it up to the dim light I examine it, *a shard of glass.* Something pungent too, strong, burning up my nostrils. *Bleach?* Cleaning product that's for sure. My face to the floor confirms it was recently cleaned. Not damp, *but I know how long that smell lingers.* Can't shake the feeling something bad's happened, something he's not telling me.

Still no sign of Jason, *damn it!* I try and quiet my mind, *deep breaths Kevin*, just like Phoebe, my shrink tells me. It ain't working. I can feel myself slipping, a concoction of anger and anxiety pulses through me...

I knew Kevin had done something bad. That's why he'd been avoiding me. Minute by minute, standing there in that apartment, standing *right there...* It all came flooding back. The smell of rust, slippery in my hands. When Kevin realised what he'd done, he disappeared leaving me to handle it. *Typical.* Kevin's strong physically, but mentally I'm the most able. Mother never understood us, the bond we had.

I told Kevin it was a bad idea, bringing a female into the mix. Told him women bring you nothing but misery! He wouldn't listen. The girl didn't want to see him again. Got fed up of his mood swings and bad temper, she couldn't understand him, she didn't *want* to understand him. *What do you expect when you kick the hornets' nest?* You get stung, that's what. Put his fist right through my table! Girl was flapping around, arms flailing, eyes were popping out of her head. She wouldn't stop screaming, which, only riled Kevin up even more. He went nuclear, throwing the furniture around, *my* furniture. What a mess, I was so angry with him. I tried to interrupt, to gain some control over the situation, but he wouldn't let me. He was too far gone. He started shaking her, willing her to be quiet. He was like a child; he didn't know what he was doing. The girl was inconsolable, I told her to calm down, but she wouldn't.

When Kevin finally realised the extent of his actions, the sheer strength of that last hit, he stepped back. Leaving me holding a lifeless, limp body in my arms.

I tried to wake her up, but it was too late, she had already stopped screaming. Thick, red droplets cascaded to the floor. The smell of blood turned my stomach, it was all too much to deal with, it was just like that night at home.

Kevin was only a kid then - I'm a good five years older than him. Mother pushed us too far, said Kevin had to go away, said I couldn't see him anymore! She said, 'When Kevin's around bad things happen.' I didn't know how to react, I felt so numb. Kevin has enough emotion for the both of us.

He was so upset. He didn't mean to hurt her, I know he didn't, but I couldn't stop him. As the knife clattered to the floor, I told him to step outside for a moment while I cleaned the place up. Of course I missed something, I must have done, I was just a kid, but I've got better since then. Better at cleaning up, better at concealing, hiding, better at pretending...

That's the difference between Kevin and I, he makes the mess and I clean it up. That's what Phoebe meant when she said I have to let him stand on his own two feet sometimes. Poor Phoebe thinks she knows us, she has no idea. Deep down, behind all that brash exterior and brute strength, there's a little boy. A scared and reckless little boy. Kevin needs me, he kills, and I clean.

It's like I've had all the pieces to the puzzle, slowly putting them back together, but when that last piece slotted in, damn that hit me like a ton of bricks. I can see her now in my head. Why she was here, how it started, why we fought. Her blood on my hands. I remember my fist going through that blasted table because she said she didn't want to see me anymore; said she couldn't handle it. *She* couldn't handle it? *She* couldn't? What about me? I *have* to handle it; I've *been* handling it! All those years, all those blasted years I've been taking care of things, and she- *she* thinks it's all about her? thought, she *thought* it was all about her. She said I was too intense, too controlling! Said I couldn't hold down a relationship, would never settle down and be happy! Said I couldn't make *her* happy! God, I got so mad, so God-damn mad! I wanted her to shut up, she wouldn't stop talking! *I had to shut her up.*

Could hear Jason's voice in the background but it wasn't enough to shake me out of it. I couldn't take her shouting and screaming at me. She was just like Jason's mother, always harpin' on at me. Telling him we couldn't be friends, always sticking the knife in! I had to shut her up too - *so I stuck my own knife in.* Jason's mother doesn't phone anymore.

Then the guilt kicked in. Not my guilt, Jason's. I could feel it, him thinking he'd let me down, like he'd failed me, just like his father had. 'You're wrong!' I said, over and over. That's the problem with Jason, he doesn't react, doesn't retaliate. Just lets it all pile up inside him until he's so depressed, so low that I have to do something bout' it! I couldn't let his father keep beatin' on him, or his mother keep calling him names! I had to help him, so I did.

He may seem cold and detached on the outside, but inside he's broken. That's when I came along, *a real friend.* Someone who would stick by him, someone who would protect him. *I had to help him.* Jason needs me you see.

Five distinct words float around in my head, *Jason's voice,* muted but comforting, 'It's going to be okay.'

'Kevin was always a loose cannon; I knew that when I first met him. As I've gotten older, I guess I didn't need him around so much, that made him sad. I felt guilty for pushing him away, for not wanting him there anymore, in my head. We used to be the best of friends.' my voice catches in my throat. 'I think I resented him for all the trouble he'd gotten us into over the years, I forgot he was only trying to help. Forgot why he appeared in the first place.' all the things he's done for me, I've never even thanked him.

'When I think about it, I owe him my life. He made all the bad people go away. Now it's my turn to pay him back, to take care of this situation, to take care of him. Please don't blame him for his mistakes, he's like a child really, he doesn't know any better. He just wanted to keep me safe the only way he knew how. Melissa was an accident. I could tell he didn't realise what he was doing, overkill, I guess. He went away for a few days after that, I didn't hear from him at all.' it all unravels from my mouth, replaying in my head. If he hadn't of seen that missing poster he'd never have remembered. I could have spared him the worry, the upset. That's why I clean so thoroughly, leaving no trace of what he's done, I'm trying to protect him.

'Please don't think badly of him, of me. We're not bad people, not really. We come as a pair, him and I. Two very different people sharing one person's body. It's like performing on stage, one minute you're in the spotlight, the next you're behind the scenes. Kevin came to me when I needed him most, a mere child. Someone for me to look out for, someone who would protect me in return. Kevin gave me a purpose, a reason to keep on living. He needs me and I need him. It's like looking in the mirror, we're the same him and I.'

The detective looks at me, completely astonished, wondering if I just made the whole thing up. *Believe me, I wish I had.* Phoebe smiles weakly as the detective's finger hovers over the record button, leaving us to await our fate as he pushes it down, ending our session.

2

THE WIDOW

REVENGE. THAT SWEET, SICKLY sensation of pain and anguish. A need for payback, a need to become the teacher of lessons; to avenge the misdeeds that have been done. Walking down the path to vengeance, hand in hand with malevolence, knowing the outcome will surely tame the restless clock ticking away in my brain. The right time, the right place. *The look on his face.* It's like he always said, 'An eye for an eye,' but now it's his sight which will be darkened as all his days fade away.

My sweet fool of a husband, how could you think this would go unnoticed? *Me, an expert in the wayward path of marriage?* Telling people day in, day out how to 'rebuild' their love from the crumbling ruins that lay before them, choking on the dust of deceit. I tell them, 'It's still possible,' *and you thought I wouldn't notice?*

The biggest fool of all, of course, *is me.* As if a degree hanging on the wall could prevent me from picking the exact example I use for my distressed clients, 'The liar, the cheat...' exhibit A for asshole.

The path now dimly lit by streetlights, I walk along unnoticed. I left my car at work of course, my alibi – my lunch break excuse for my absence from the office. Not that any of them care, tossers. I'm the only one that does any bloody work in that place. Oh I've been waiting for this day. They'll all care then won't they?

when I'm too bereaved to function, too distraught to work. A nice break will do me a world of good – paid leave, of course.

Trees rhythmically sway in the autumnal breeze, September leaves crunch beneath my shallow footsteps as I near my home, Eighty-six Riverbed Drive. *The excitement my dead husband will bring to this close-knit neighbourhood!* Oh they'll all be looking out their windows then, won't they? through their unsightly nets, with their mug of tea in one hand and a digestive in the other. 'What a shock,' they'll say. 'He was such a nice man,' even though half the street despised him anyway. I expect I'll be inundated with dodgy homemade lasagne's or overbaked apple pies - assuming I've resorted to microwave meals in front of the telly due to grief. 'You're wasting away,' they'll tell me. Oh yes, I've thought about it all great detail. My plan is simple yet genius, right now, my husband will be on his way home with his mistress. *How safe he feels thinking I'm at work until six.* Just enough time for him to wrap up his adultery for the evening - only to pick up where they left off tomorrow. *Unbeknown to you my darling, I left early.*

I position myself rather awkwardly in the closet – *surely you won't be tempted to hang your clothes up, will you darling?* No, they'll be crumpled in a heap on the floor. To think, I ironed them so nicely as well…

They frolic their way up the stairs to our bedroom - no need to be quiet as the wife is not here. But here I am, waiting, anticipating, *in the dark.*

I slap my hand over my mouth to quiet my deep inhaling, trapping the stale air in my lungs, the last of the somewhat 'clean' air I can find, knowing now that the oxygen outside of this dank closet is fetid with adultery and lust.

Cold metal rests in my palm, a 9mm semi-automatic, *his* gun. My fingers stroke the trigger. It's hard to see in the dark, my heart pounding in my chest - *they'll hear that for sure.* I can see them through the slit in the closet door, just visible. His hands dancing up and down her body making bile rise in my throat.

Our house, our room, *our bed.* I should burst out now and end them both!

No, not yet, it has to be the right time. Waiting for this however, is testing my patience. It has to be how I imagined it, how I planned. The look on his face as the bullet grazes past him, heading straight for its intended victim, *her.*

I've watched enough crime shows to avoid any rookie mistakes. I shoot her, then stage his suicide. What if it doesn't work? It *will* work, it *has* to work. All those months of planning, I cannot slip up.

I don't blame her of course, she's just as under his spell as I was. What fools we've both been! Well I'm doing you a favour honey - *he was never going to leave me anyway.* She fits the profile exactly: slim, sexy, provocative – the perfect mistress. Oh, how funny it is to be in this scenario myself! I make a living from coaching dysfunctional couples and tormented wives, yet I finally find myself here, in this closet, preparing myself to avenge my marriage. Everything I worked for, gave up, sacrificed, for what? *For him.* My husband, who looks great on paper but managed to fool even me, an expert! *I could just shoot him now.* No! It has to be her first, I can't bear the screams that will escape from her pretty little mouth. *I want him to know what I'm capable of.*

The police will assume it's a classic tale of the impetuous mistress, the 'bunny boiler' who demanded he leave his wife. They get into an argument, he pulls out the gun from the bedside cabinet, there's a struggle – whoops, she's dead. He can't cope with prison (he wouldn't like the food), considers fleeing the country, but remembers he doesn't have the balls (or the brains) to flee a crime scene. So what's the alternative? bang, bang, there he goes as well. *It's almost too easy.*

They're both naked now, entangled. It's disgusting and thrilling at the same time that, in the midst of their adultery, they have no idea I'm here, hiding, ready to pounce, *ready to kill.*

Nearly time. Just a little longer, let them really lose themselves – it will be more devastating, how he really had no idea. Perhaps I'll see embarrassment in his eyes as I face him, revealing myself. The gun gripped in both hands now, I slowly slip it between the gap in the door, pushing it discreetly, still so undetected as it doesn't make a sound. *Good thing I greased the door hinge beforehand.*

I line her head up with my gun. He can't see me until she's dead. Ready? three, two, one- BANG! The noise deafens me, then comes the second blow, finishing my ears off. The blood splatter up the wall seems almost artistic, painted by an artist which is not me. The gun feeble in my hand, cold, unused…

The muddled bodies go limp and motionless, he collapses onto her. My hand finds my mouth in the dark as I retreat further into the closet. Not me, not me, *it wasn't me?* I fumble around with the gun - the safety is still on! *Amateur.* So, whodunit?

A black mass blocks the remainder of the light from the closet. *A man.* His heavy footing echoes through the room as he checks both corpses – dead as a dodo; unequivocally deceased.

He did it, this man, whoever he is! Whatever his

reasons for killing my husband and his mistress, (her husband perhaps?) I don't care. I'm almost grateful (almost, because he has denied me the pleasure of my plan), thankful for his part in this. *He is the killer, I am innocent.* I have to shut my mouth up to stop the laughter from escaping. How hilarious, the two of us, planning this illicit crime - my unknown accomplice! Like parallel lines running alongside each other, never meeting, until the penultimate finale. *Bravo!*

I slip back into the clothing rails, engulfed by my dead husband's suits, shrouding me from the scene of the crime. Here I will remain until my dark angel has disappeared. Then I will slip out the back door, undetected, back to my desk at work to eventually discover I am a widow when I return home - his life insurance mine for the taking! *The perfect crime.*

I wipe a false tear from my eye as I practice mourning the death of my bastard husband.

3

THE DOLLHOUSE

SECRETS, EVERY FAMILY HAS THEM. Those deep, dark troubles that fester in your mind like a plague, haunting you, controlling you. *A thorn in one's side.*

I wish it wasn't this way. Wish none of it had ever happened, but it has, and it's happened to me.

My memory isn't the most reliable of sources

right now, but I think that's a blessing in disguise. There are a lot of instances I don't want to remember – *like how I got here.*

There's a sadness in his eyes, a sorrow, a hurting. Maybe you'll figure it out for yourself one day, what he hides here, but I pray you never will. There's only one way you're getting in this place, but you'd better know the way back out.

Peter's no monster, not really, not when you know his story. He's just a dark-haired man of average height, mid-thirties with sloping shoulders and Clark Kent glasses he'd be useless without – Peter's no superhero though. He told me once about his little sister. Meg she was called, *Meg-Smeg.* They were close, although he was ten years older than she was. Peter built her a dollhouse one Christmas, just like the one in the shop, the one their mother couldn't afford. A boozer he told me; said she didn't have her priorities right. One night, Peter had snuck out late to meet his friends, it's what he found when he got home that still haunts him.

Smoke, lots and lots of smoke had escaped under the front door. Bright light blazed through the kitchen window. Peter ran in and climbed the stairs. The smoke had already engulfed most of the house.

'Meg?' He screamed as he reached his sister's door – it was locked, so was his mother's. Beads of sweat formed on his forehead as he pounded desperately at the door. Peter and his fifteen-year-old lanky body kicked at Meg's door until it flew off the hinges. There she was just there on the bed. He carried her in his arms. Floppy, *like one of her dolls.*

The fire had reached the bottom of the stairs as they made it down. A neighbour had called the fire department. The shrill noise of the fire engine was the last memory he could recall. Everything after that was a blur. His mother had deliberately started the fire, she locked herself and her children in their rooms – thinking Peter was home too. Meg was asthmatic, she died that night of smoke inhalation. His mother had topped herself.

He only told me once, but that story chilled me so

much it stays there, imprinted in my brain as if it were my own. Part of me wishes he'd just snap out of this and go live a normal life. You know, get married, have a few kids? Peter isn't settled, hasn't been since then and I don't think he'll ever be. It's not like he hasn't had women interested in him, I mean he's rather attractive – in a mysterious, you-look-like-a-normal-guy, kind of way. Only, Peter isn't normal, and I don't think he'll ever be. Yes, Peter's had dates – *I was one of them.*

It was a casual encounter, I worked as a barista at a coffee shop in town. Peter used to come in every morning for his usual, triple, venti, soy, no foam, latte (yes, he's very particular). I guess that's why I never gave him much attention before, I thought he was just another arrogant coffee snob, and I was fine with that. One Friday evening he appeared as I was closing – very unusual for him considering the time, asked me if I wanted to go for dinner one night. I should have trusted my gut because I had a strange feeling about him, but what can I say? *the man intrigued me.* Dinner one night turned into three dinners and lunch. I guess he was having a go at being a normal guy. At least that's what I told myself, and not that he had this planned all along - *although part of me believes he did.* The stupid part is, arrogant coffee-snob Peter began to grow on me and the more we talked the more he opened up. Maybe I have a way of bringing people out of themselves, getting to know them in a way others never bother to. Doing so was my downfall that night, *the night I came here.*

Peter's a good cook - make no mistake about that, although I've no idea who taught him to cook (certainly wasn't his mother). We talked over a bottle of vintage Malbec, (wine snob too) and what was probably the most delicious meal I've ever had (wine may or may not have had something to do with it). Some sort of slow cooked pulled pork - which, *I was told,* is a great companion of the wine (I had no idea what he was talking about). Anyway, that's when I wish I'd bitten my tongue. He'd mentioned his sister and I asked him how old she was. He explained, reluctantly at first, choosing his words carefully until eventually they all came tumbling out his mouth like a verbal avalanche. I was glued to my chair, chilled. *How could a mother do that to her children?* I felt guilty for judging him so harshly. Came to the conclusion he was cold and distant because of the pain he must feel inside. He grew nervous then, fidgety, as if waiting for me to notice something.

I thought my drowsiness was due to the 'deep bodied and robust' inky slosh in my glass, but I should have noticed it sooner. The way he rearranged the cutlery on the table; how he folded and unfolded the napkins. He was nervous, and not in a first-date kind of way. A misty haze obscured my vision as the glass left my hand, its fragile body smashed at my feet.

I remember when I woke up, I felt paralysed. My body frozen upright in a wooden chair sat in a room full of objects, objects that didn't belong to me. There's one object in the corner that still haunts me most, *the dollhouse.* There's a family in there; a mother and her two daughters. Tiny, china dolls. Fragile things I could crush so easily in one hand. Seemingly flawless, but if you look closely enough, you'll notice the cracks.

I call the smallest doll Megan - like Peter's sister. She reminds me of someone, but I can't think who. *Poor little Meg-Smeg.*

I must have dozed off. Maybe I'm still dreaming, but I can feel my body alive again with sensation. My fingers twitch slowly as I try to gain control of them. *Clench fist, unclench, repeat.* How long until he comes back with the next dosage?

I must sound relatively calm for someone in my situation. I suppose it's because any effort to escape, or even scream, is futile when your body is about as useful as a sack of potatoes with eyes (glad to know I've still got my sense of humour). My legs extend out beneath me. I enjoy the stretch, the movement. You know? normal motor functions. Blood rushes to every available destination in my body as I stand. Arms above my head, giving neck a little twist too. *I wish I could go outside.* Feel the sunlight on my skin. Breeze in my hair. All I've got is this stupid fake window with a stupid beach scene. I don't even like the beach! Don't like getting sand in my shoes, or in my eyes for that matter - although that doesn't sound half bad right now.

I'm still a bit groggy, stumbling around like I've had one too many tequilas, but I'm mobile and that's the main thing. *Is he home?* I can't hear anything upstairs. No footsteps as he potters around.

I feel more alert than I have been in a few days, maybe now is as good a time as any to bust outta' here. The door would be an obvious choice for escape, I can't imagine he'd have left it unlocked - although, considering my usual vegetative state that's probably exactly what he's done. My heart rate quickens as I reach for the door handle. *Can it really be as easy as just walking out of here?* Haven't you ever seen, Escape from Alca – *it opens.* I swing the door back and forth a few times just to make sure I'm not hallucinating (another side effect of Peter's potion). It was unlocked the whole time!

To my surprise, a corridor awaits me outside my cell door. It's much larger down here than I was expecting. Whitewash walls with grey tile flooring. Not the dark, dank, cellar I had pictured. My body freezes on the spot when I notice her. A girl, not much younger than me, practically floats along the hall towards me. *I'm not the only one down here?* I feel physically sick. He's probably had a bunch of us here the entire time!

My voice hushed, 'Hey you, pigtails,' the girl looks my way, as high as a kite, 'It's okay, I'm going to get us out of here!'

She smiles as I grab her arm, a look of confusion on her sweet face, 'What game are we playing Sophie?'

How does she know my name? Confused, I lead her along the corridor. We pass several other doors along the way. Are these rooms soundproof or what? I never heard a thing. Okay, game plan, need to get out of here before he comes back.

'What's your name?' practically carrying her now.

'Lucy,' her voice as quiet as a mouse.

'Okay Lucy, do you know if he's home?'

She gives me that dopey confused look again, 'Who?'

'Peter of course, is he home?' We creep slowly to a flight of stairs. They must lead to the rest of the house. What is this place, *a dollhouse?*

Loopy Lucy stops in her tracks, 'Who's Peter?'

I don't have time for this. Maybe I should just leave the kid and run, she'll only slow me down. No, couldn't have that on my conscience, but what about the other girls? What would you do? You'd save them, wouldn't you? You wouldn't just leave them here, with *him*.

'Come on Lucy, we have to go.' I say as we start running together now, our bare feet slapping at the cold floor with every impact.

There's a door at the top of the stairs, pushing it ajar I peek through the gap, 'Coast is clear, come on.'

'Sophie, we're not allowed to be here.'

'Well it's the only way out.' my voice a hushed whisper as I hear someone coming toward us.

'Sophie, I don't want to go, I want to stay.' she says, I notice the teddy bear in her hand. A matted old thing with an eye missing and various holes in its body. She looks only about sixteen, which turns my stomach even more. *Sicko.*

Resisting her feeble attempt to escape my grasp – she's only a weakling, I drag her out the door with me before realising it's too late. *He's coming.* He adjusts his glasses before plummeting toward us, but he stops before the three of us can collide.

'Sophie? Lucy? How'd you get up here?' It's not anger I sense in his voice, but something else, concern.

'I told her I didn't want to come, she made me!'

'Alright Lucy, go on off and play.' He ushers her away, 'I can take care of Sophie.'

Play? Is he twisted in the head? 'You can't keep me here you sicko!' I scream at him. He gets a strong grip on my wrists to stop me thrashing at his face.

'I know what you've done,' my voice is raspy and strained, 'I know you're keeping other girls here too!'

'Sophie, I'm sorry,' something pricks in my arm,

'you're not well, you need rest.' No. *No!* I'm shouting but the words don't come out my mouth. I slouch into his arms as the lights go off.

My head is strangely light and fuzzy. I open my eyes to the blazing white room and see Peter sat in the corner, *watching me.* I have to get out of this mad house!

'Sophie, what can you remember from that night?' I may be drowsy but at least I can still move.

'What night?'

Peter steps toward me, 'The night of the fire,' he pauses, 'the night your sister died.'

Fire? Sister? He's got it all wrong, it's *his* fire, *his* sister!

'You know it wasn't your fault Sophie, you couldn't have saved her.'

'Stop it!' my throat as dry as a bone, 'You're lying! It's your sister who died, I don't have a sister!'

'Sophie your sister, Megan died when you were fifteen.'

'You're lying!' I'm screaming now.

'Your mother tried to kill you all.'

'Doctor Peterson maybe you should let her sleep for a while,' a man I hadn't noticed before is stood by the door, a syringe in his hand, 'she's very distressed,' *he's in on it too?*

Peter ignores the man, 'Sophie, you're here because of what happened that night.' his voice is softer now, strangely soothing, 'You've created this fantasy where I'm the monster because you can't come to terms with what's happened.' he sits beside me, 'You're still in denial.' *No!*

'But you poisoned me! My drink...' I can barely string a sentence together.

'Sophie, it isn't true.' he looks at me like I'm a little lost sheep, 'It's all in your head.' *He's crazy.*

'You can't accept why you're here, why you need help.' his eyes fixed on me, 'You've contrived this elaborate story where you've been abducted, locked in a basement.'

He's lying! Isn't he? 'The drugs...'

'To keep you docile, you're a danger to yourself and to the other patients,' *patients?* 'You've been here six months now Sophie, we thought you were improving, but today's little incident,' he sighs, 'well its clear the treatment isn't working.' *Treatment?*

'Where the hell am I?' my heart bursts in my chest.

'Pembrook Psychiatric Institution.'

'No Peter, it's not true,' that same prickly feeling in my arm again, 'you, *you* did this!' A soft touch brushes the hair from my face. Numbness — my old friend, washes over me again.

'Megan?' *Your laughter, it fills my head.*

'Shh, that's it, you sleep now.' the other man says.

The last thing I see is Peter peering over me, a blank expression on his face,

'Sophie, *I'm your psychiatrist.*'

4

THE CRIMSON BRIDES

THE CRIMSON TIDE BENEATH MY bare feet, now a mere puddle as it's soaked up by the ends of my tattered dress. My second face melting away with every thrash, revealing my bare flesh, mascara running, filling every crevice, every scar of my skin. He doesn't hold back this time – every hit critical. The waiter? No, *the speech!* Must have been it, must have set him off. I curse every word from my brother-in-law's mouth, 'Married the wrong brother!' *pig.* I laughed of course until I saw his face change, like my mother used to say about my father, 'He's got the devil in his eyes,' that look. *What a way to end our wedding day!* Pain tears through my entire being, my sight fades to black as he delivers the last fatal blow – *there's only so many bones you can bear breaking.*

The antique clock on the wall reads six-forty am. Did I crawl back to bed or did he put me here? My skin is as cold and as hard as stone, rainbow coloured welts cover the surface – *I look like a child's drawing!* I should make a run for it now, annul this sham of a marriage, have him locked up. He's gone too far.

I try to rise up, but my body is heavy, I am weak. *Where is he?* Making me breakfast no doubt, arranging tulips. I won't forgive him this time. Up I go, *left foot, right foot.* My appearance in the mirror is unrecognisable to me. I throw the contents of my makeup bag to the floor - *as if all the porcelain in the world could cover this mess up.* He's gone too far this time.

To discover he is not in the kitchen, nowhere in fact, makes the excruciating trip down the stairs a waste. *Has he run first? Unable to face me? Left me for dead?* No, this isn't right, where's my penitent letter? My abundance of love? *My husband?*

Water is no relief to my dried-out throat, the arctic temperature of the house makes the water practically Siberian. The last bitter drop of water hits the back of my throat, that's when I notice the tulips. *Yellow, like the morning sun.* Always yellow, since our first date. I sigh deeply. So, where is he? My nose to a single tulip and I can smell nothing. Perhaps he damaged that too.

It isn't until I nearly trip over it, that I realise I am still in my wedding dress. I mean, I must have noticed earlier, when I woke up, surely? I must have noticed the colour, the smell of stale blood. My once beautiful dress, nothing fancy – just like me, now a shabby robe hanging from my bony frame, stained by the blood of my naivety. Of course he wasn't going to change, *silly girl.*

I awake in darkness. It takes a while for my eyes to adjust to the fact the room is just dimly lit, daylight escaping from my home. *Escape.* My head pounds with the drum beat of a heavy metal band. Did I fall asleep? I am again on the bed, clock ticking away. Six-forty am? This can't be right, it's morning again, not evening. Perhaps I'm more concussed that I thought.

The bedroom seems different now, the same, but different. Paint peeling off the walls, damp, mildew air, mould spores on the curtains. I try the latch on the window, desperate for some fresh air, but it won't budge. *Stupid thing!*

I'm weary and tired, although I've slept through most of yesterday. 'Damn!' My heart flees my chest as a bird smashes into the window. A tiny sparrow, no bigger than the palm of my hand, slides down the glass and onto the ground below. *He was heading straight for me, poor thing.*

I realise I've not eaten in what must be two days, nor have I had any desire to, but perhaps it would help. I catch myself in the mirror again, less colourful than before, paler perhaps? It's then I notice something odd, a band of gold sitting on the bedside table, *his wedding ring*. I slip its companion off my skeletal finger and place it beside his, *you did this*.

Something catches my attention, a noise, talking? No, *footsteps*. As I stumble to the top of the stairs I'm almost certain I'll collide with him. He's nowhere to be seen. *But I heard him?* An aria of laughter erupts from the bedroom, *a woman's voice*. But I was just in there?

Peering my head into the room, everything appears changed. The peeling paint now a bright, sunshine yellow. The furniture rearranged, things not where I left them. That's when I see him. Arms wrapped around a slim blonde, younger than me, prettier. *They're laughing!* Rage spreads through me like a forest fire, *how could you!* Something stops me from entering the room, *glass.* Cold, hard glass, too hard to put my fists through. *A window?* The window I tried to open this morning; I'm outside looking in! I'm locked out!

As I back away from the window, from the house, everything starts to become clearer. I look down at my feet, they're not on the ground, in fact, they're barely feet at all, just wisps of air as I practically float outside the house. Outside *my* house. I can still see them in the bedroom, I want to reach out and scream, to pound at the window! Though what would be the point? *They can't see me at all.*

I stare for what feels like an eternity, or has it already been that long? Someone calls to me,

'Lauren,' I turn to see a woman stood beside me, 'it's okay.' I recognise her long auburn hair, hazel eyes,

'Sarah.' *my husband's ex-wife.* She's wearing a similar stained lace dress, a gaping hole in her stomach…

I shake my head slowly, nervously, *but she's dead!* I place my hand on the window and watch it fade away, a glistening tear rolls off my cheek, *I'm* dead. *We're* dead.

Here we stand, hand in hand, on the outside looking into our former home. Two alabaster angels, victims of the same man - the devil in the gentleman's coat, *waiting for the next crimson bride.*

5

A Night at the Marmont

DUSK FALLS ON SUNSET BOULEVARD, the cars still roaring down the street louder than ever. Atop the glitzy sunset strip, the Chateau Marmont sits peering down upon Hollywood, its eyes open wide for a scandal. *The scandal however, if you look close enough, takes place inside…*

The heiress, Miss Josephine Rogers sips precariously on her dry martini, her eyes fixated on the clock as if seeing straight through it. She occupies the lounge room, dimly lit and hazy, with its oriental rugs and grandiose ceilings, playing with the pearls around her neck.

Unlike other heiresses in her circle, Josephine doesn't care for money. To her, it's a convenience and nothing more. To her father however, money is something he likes to hold above people's heads, it makes him feel privileged and powerful. *Power in the hands of the wrong man, can make him do dastardly things.*

Johannes Brand, a rather miserable and pale looking fellow, sits in the chair by the fire. A Scandinavian chap of very few words. His fidgeting catches the attention of Josephine, he glares back at her emotionless and cold. With a tremendous sigh he slumps back in the chair, pouring himself another large glass of brandy. A stern looking woman sits at the far side of the room, her withered lips pressed to a cigarette, Rose Randall. If ever there was a woman more scorned by love, it was her. Rose was the type to notice everything, *but there are a few things Josephine would prefer went unnoticed.*

The Chateau Marmont is the perfect hideaway for many affairs. A place free of judgement, where the walls hold secrets and the staff turn a blind eye. Josephine felt somewhat safe here, *as safe as someone like her could be in a place like this.* Her father had ruled her all her life, she felt as though he owned her, and that is exactly how he treated her, like an investment. A man ruled by money, Walter Rogers has never got himself into a situation he couldn't buy himself out of. He was a cold, calculating man with a poisonous tongue.

Josephine grips her martini glass so tightly it ought to crack in her hand. A sickly feeling rises up from her stomach, but it isn't fear that consumes her, *it's hatred.* She hates her father, the control he exercises over her, making every decision for her. The ring on her left-hand sparkles in the light. He even chose for her a husband! A wealthy, respected young man of course, *Lawrence Carlisle.* A rather handsome man, but with a bad attitude and an equally as bad temper. There was no way she was going through with the wedding, and her father was a fool for believing so. She had grown to be quite calculating herself, as well as smart and cunning – she learned from the best! For the past three months she's been transferring money from her father's account overseas for a company he'd invested in - *a company that doesn't exist.* No longer would she be her father's property, or even his daughter. Once he finds out she's gone he'll write her out of his will. Not that it will matter, she's already embezzled enough of his money to ensure she lives comfortably for the rest of her life.

Not long now, almost time for her and her beloved to run away together. She smiles up from her glass as a young man appears in the doorway. His cheeks flushed and plump, his smile not that of a rich man's, not smug and proud, but humble. His suit not the work of a fine tailors, and his watch, which had belonged to his father, doesn't tick. Josephine leaps from her chair to greet the boy,

'Oh Henry!' Wrapping her arms around her beloved, placing a kiss on his cheek. Josephine, now very aware she's being watched, turns to Rose to introduce the stranger, 'This is my dear childhood friend, Henry Moore.'

Unconvinced, Rose smiles back half-heartedly. In Hollywood, it was common knowledge that Josephine Rogers was engaged to be married to a rich and debonair young man, and not of course, to this fortuneless buck who doesn't have two dimes to rub together. Josephine leads Henry out onto the terrace where they're safe from prying eyes. She wraps her arms around his shoulders, resting her delicate wrists upon the nape of his neck and kisses him. Unbeknown to them, Rose has the perfect view of the pair from her seat in the lounge room. Getting up, she draws the curtains, shutting them out as she swipes a match to her cigarette. Who is she to interfere with the hearts of young lovers? *Love itself is a tyrant, and these two are playing with fire.*

Johannes sits alone outside on the terrace, a glass of brandy, a cigar, and a pen, all interchangeably trading places in his hands as he writes in a journal. A waiter attempts to top up his glass, but he wafts him away incessantly.

Josephine and Henry occupy a table in the corner of the room, she places her hand over his. Something is on her mind, that much is obvious to him, 'My darling, what is it?' he asks, brushing her cheek.

His touch startles her, 'It's nothing love,' she pauses, choosing her words carefully as she lowers her voice, 'it's just, I feel many eyes upon me.'

Henry, unsure of what she means leans towards her, 'Do you mean you know these people?'

'No, *but they know me.'* She catches the eye of Johannes Brand as he comes in from the terrace. Something falls to the floor, his journal. The waiter hurries to his side and reaches down to help retrieve it.

'Keep your hands to yourself!' Johannes roars, the whole room turns in his direction. He swipes up the book himself and hurries away.

'Let's do it tonight,' Henry says, not checking to see who is around to hear, 'Josephine we've waited long enough!' She hushes him, desperate to shut him up,

'Henry, please, keep your voice down.'

The two stand at the top of the stairs, unaware of a pair of eyes watching them. *He has grown too impatient.* They've both waited so long to be together, and part of her very much wished to leave right there and then, but she was no coward. She wanted to be the one to tell her father what a fool he had been with his money, what she'd done. That the company he had been investing in was all in her name! That's the problem with these wealthy men, she thought, *they are stupid.* He never even read the contract - she would get the lot!

'Soon Henry, very soon.'

The night had grown dark, but the party lived on all along the Sunset Strip. Hollywood was more alive than ever! The curtains in Miss Roger's room however, closed to the outside world forever as the clock struck an un-Godly hour.

The door creaked open, it was three o'clock in the morning and she was fast asleep. Henry had left an hour or so before, creeping back to his own room unnoticed. At least, *that's what he thought.* A dark figure entered the room and made its way slowly toward Josephine's bed. The figure lingered for a moment, hovering beside the restful heiress. Silence, except for the sound of heavy breathing. An engagement ring slides from her delicate finger, still she doesn't stir. The figure strokes her hair, softly, before grabbing a fistful and yanking it tight.

'Wha- who…who are you?' her heart pounds in her chest, her voice a whisper in the night. She reaches for the bedside lamp but in her fumbling knocks it to the floor, its smash rings out through the night. The figure holds her down as she tries desperately to get up. Both faces now illuminated by the moonlight, Josephine gasps, recognising the face before her. There is little time to scream before a dagger comes plunging through her chest.

Rose looked on as police flooded the Marmont, *news reporters are such vultures.* She was shocked of course, but experience had taught her not to get involved. There was no doubt as to why Josephine was killed, *didn't take a detective to work that out.* Rose did feel somewhat guilty however, as though it could have been prevented somehow. Last night, she noticed someone watching Josephine and Henry in the hallway.

She recognised him instantly from the papers, watched him slip into the room of Miss Rogers. *But who was she to interfere with the hearts of young lovers?* The man she saw last night, was of course the young debonair, Lawrence Carlisle, *Josephine's fiancé.*

Rose shut the door to her room and lit a cigarette. She lifted something to the air, admiring its brilliance as it shone in the light. *What a beautiful ring*, she thought, such a generous reward for keeping her mouth shut...

6

HELLO DIARY, MY OLD FRIEND

SOMETIMES IT'S NICE TO LOOK back through the eyes of a child. Your eyes when they saw nothing but innocence, when they believed in anything and had that energy, that curiosity to know and see everything. It was a refreshing little trip for me going through some old boxes in the attic. Old drawings from primary school, a ton of those necklaces we used to make out of pasta and string, a few locks of my hair from different years – all which mum had kept safely together in an old brown box. The best thing of all though, was when I stumbled upon an old childhood diary of mine, the one with the blue furry dog on the cover and the tiny little padlock that required an equally tiny metal key. My surprise when I discovered it was already unlocked, an invitation to the past! Welcome, my ten-year-old self. The mind of a dreamer, singer, actress, writer - whatever she wanted to be.

Flicking through the pages I took note that she wrote religiously for a few weeks, then stopped for a while, only to re-emerge a few days later (a pattern I admittedly still possess). Each time apologising (to the diary) for having gone rogue. 'Diary' it would seem, had become somewhat of an old friend and was treated as such, *'Sorry I've not got much to say today Diary,'* or *'I promise to write in you tomorrow.'* At times, Diary was a confession box or a hot-off-the-press tabloid containing all the latest neighbourhood kids gossip, *'Georgia ACTUALLY kissed Cory!!!!'* The drama emphasised by the various capitalised words and ten thousand exclamation marks. I found myself laughing at certain entries,

'Dear Diary, today me, Georgia and Cody went down the hill. I know I'm not allowed to go that far, so don't tell mum! Shh. We found a car that was left in the car park, it was all smashed up and the windows were missing, so we climbed inside to investigate.'

In some ways, Diary was like an older sister or a cool aunt, someone I could tell anything to and who wouldn't tell me off. There are days when Little Me talked about the 'dens' she'd made with her friends. She was always out playing, claiming barren lands and overgrown bushes as her own secret hideout - *all specifically grown-up free zones.* They were places she could smuggle her lunch into and play make-believe with her fellow pirates, explorers, and vampires. Many times, she tested the boundaries of where she was allowed to go. Each time going that little bit further until it all got a bit too scary out there, and she and her friends decided they preferred their usual stomping ground. I remember the thudding sound her shoes made as she raced home when the streetlights came on in the winter, marking the end of their day,

'See ya later alligator!'

'In a while crocodile!'

Their laughter echoing under the red-brick arch that led to their cul-de-sac. Of course, there were times Little Me and her friends would fall out or when the group would split up and declare war on the other. But for the most part they all got along well, all taking it in turns to go play at each other's houses or have sleepovers.

Summertime was always the best of course, they even started their own car washing business – *although, splitting two pounds per car between five of them did become the cause of many disagreements.* They decided to cut their losses and find a new business venture - the lemonade stand. Then came the garden sales, Little Me put most of her belongings in the front garden only to decide nothing was for sale when someone came to buy anything.

Probably the most fun of all though, was the water balloon fights. Overfilling balloons and carefully sneaking up on friends to fire them at their unsuspecting heads - *only to get an even bigger one thrown back at you as payment!*

Another diary entry brings with it a rather unpleasant smell, something that still makes me feel a little sick at the thought of it - the custard pie fight,

'Dear Diary, today we had a custard pie fight in the park for Megan's birthday, it was so GROSS. Mum couldn't get the custard out of my hair for days and all my clothes had to be thrown as they smelled yuk. It was good fun though, but I did get a custard pie thrown in my face - even the grown-ups joined in!'

Yes, suffice to say I never, *ever* participated in a

custard pie fight again. There are also those embarrassing memories, which, at the time seemed like a good idea but now just cause me to deny I was *that* child. The child who sang at the talent show every year. I was Kylie Minogue for the first few, with my white jumpsuit and singing to, *Can't Get You Out of My Head* (I still cringe at the thought). Then came my punk rock stage where everything was a shade of black or grey and I wore those baggy combat trousers with the long strands of fabric hanging on by Velcro (I still don't know what you call those). Kylie was no more, and it was Avril Lavigne's *Sk8r Boi* that I sang and played air guitar to in front of the *entire* school. I must say I was quite the performer back then.

Then came the day all fathers – in this case, mothers – would dread, that first 'crush',

'Dear Diary, the new boy at school is called Sam, he is soooooo cute! All the girls fancy him, but they can forget it because he's going out with Rhea now. I play football with him at break time and he said I'm

good! I only play it because he does. Shh don't tell!'

How quickly that progressed to the next entry,

'DIARY!! I am the LUCKIEST girl in the whole world. Sam asked me to be his girlfriend! Mum says I'm too young to have a boyfriend and that I'm not allowed to kiss him – yuk, as if!'

Little Me talks about the notes he would send her in class — some of them are still stuck to the pages of the diary, little stick figure people drawn in blue ink in various stick-like poses, hugging or holding hands. Other little notes with almost illegible handwriting scrawled on scraps of paper with messages like, 'Will you marry me?' And 'I will love you forever and ever and ever!' I remember how Little Me would be sat talking on the phone to him every evening after school – as if they hadn't spent enough time together already. They used to hug each other before they left school every day too. A whole week later and Romeo and

Juliet were officially no more...

'Dear Diary, me and Sam are OVER. I found out he was two timing me with Maisie!!!! I thought he was acting different because he stopped hugging me after school. Mum said she's going to have a word with his parents!'

I remember not wanting to go to school because I didn't want to see him – or Maisie! A few days later though and it was nice to see Little Me was back to writing about what she had for lunch and that Big Dave's GIANT dog Monty had done a wee all up Megan's leg.

My head is filled with snippets of a life I once lived, playing in my mind as if I were watching a home movie. I find it interesting how these memories never came to me until I stumbled upon that old diary. As if they were stored away, never being found until times like these. I'd forgotten how much fun my childhood was, nothing to worry about but trivial things that didn't really matter all that much. I look back at how far I've come since then, all the real issues I've had to face, all that's happened since those sunny summer days in the park, how people have come and gone. I'd like to tell Little Me that it will all turn out alright in the end. There's someone I'd like to speak to most of all though, an old friend of mine...

I pick up the blue furry book, a sudden yearning to speak to Diary once more. To tell her all that's happened since my last entry where my little brother fell asleep in his jelly.

I open the diary to a new page, its edges crisp and curling slightly. My pen scratches the page with eagerness and excitement, all these years later and my words still flow freely and effortlessly as if no time at all has passed. I begin the next chapter of my life with two very important words,

'Dear Diary,'

7

LIFE AFTER DEATH

ALL I REMEMBER, IS THE SOUND of metal crushing, and brakes screeching. Then it all went black.

I woke up on the ceiling. The room was different. It had a kind of pinkish hue to it, a purple haze. Something was off, I knew it was the same room, but things were in the wrong place, the door was on the opposite side of the room and the bed was facing the other way. I tried to wake myself up, thrashing my arms and legs around. *It didn't work.*

I looked down at the bed to see someone laying there, asleep. I looked closer, horrified at what I saw. The person, the girl in my bed, *was me.* Suddenly, I started hurtling away from my body as if something was dragging me. I couldn't breathe. *What an awful dream!* I thought. That's when I felt it, a hand on my shoulder, stopping me from moving any further. A voice spoke to me, it wasn't coming from the room, but within me, though it wasn't my voice,

'You're making it too difficult' it said.

I didn't understand. Then it spoke again, I heard the words, 'be still.' I don't know why, but somehow, I trusted this voice. I stopped trying to fight my way out of it and hushed my mind. Slowly, I began to float to the floor until my feet were on solid ground. All the haze before had faded and colours came magically to life. Everything in the room had returned to how it should be the sun was streaming in through the curtains. I smelled the sweet smell of roses beside my bed and the muffled commotion of people going past my door in the hallway.

I was relieved, until I saw my body still there on the bed. *Am I dead?* I thought. Then the voice appeared again,

'Think of a time you felt safe,' an odd request of course, but the image was conjured in my mind. I thought of the Lighthouse we used to visit when I was a kid, I used to go down to the beach and climb the rocks – even though my Dad told me it wasn't safe. One summer I slipped and fell onto the one below, then the one below that, until I was hanging on for dear life. The water was thrashing about beneath me; I was terrified because I couldn't swim. I'd never seen a man move so fast. I watched my dad as he heroically leapt from rock to rock until he was there pulling me up. I cried my little eyes out whilst he just scooped me up in his arms and held on to me tight, 'close one kiddo.' *He never even shouted at me.*

Suddenly, I was no longer in my room, I was

there, on that beach in my dad's arms. I didn't understand, 'How can I be here again? how can I be that little girl again?' I was looking through her eyes, *my eyes,* the eyes of a child.

The voice replied, 'You were never not her, just as you will never not be you in ten years' time, or ten years after that.'

Baffled, 'I don't get it, how can I be experiencing this?'

'You can experience anything you wish, there is nothing that you cannot have, do, or be, it is all a matter of perspective.' the voice continued,

'You, as humans believe that is all you are, that you are limited to what you can experience, but it is not so.'

I simply did not understand, how could I be out of my body, not dead, and now experiencing this event from my childhood? 'Please, explain this to me in a way I can better understand.'

Imagine yourself in ten years' time, how would you like your life to be?' the voice spoke again. I pictured a nice house, a happy family, a loving husband, a good job, and the voice showed me that it was possible. There I was again, another version of myself, a bit older, much wiser. I wished to remain there, to skip whatever I had to face between now and then. I looked happy. *I felt happy.* Was that how my life would be? Could I really have all that? Those questions floated around in my mind. I felt somewhat optimistic, excited, but I was still afraid of something. In the back of my mind, I felt as though I did not deserve good things. I did not deserve the money, or the happy home. *Would I ever get over that belief?*

'Now,' the voice said, 'think of something you're afraid of,' and just like that I was drowning in the sea, water choking me, stinging my eyes as I thrashed about trying to stay afloat. I was terrified, it was my worst nightmare, and no one was around to save me! I remembered those first few words, 'be still.' I stopped moving and sure enough I sank, but I hushed my mind once more, this time I thought of something else. I thought of a beach, with soft, white sand, palm trees and a warm sea breeze. Suddenly, the waves crashed about, moving me with them as I washed up on the shore. The sand was soft beneath me, I remained still for a while, recovering from my ordeal.

I asked myself, 'If this is a dream, then how come it feels so real?' To which the voice appeared once again, 'Because it is not a dream, you are still alive.'

'How can this be?'

'You have left your body; you are no longer confined to the restrictions of the human mind.' I listened carefully, '*Here* you manifest things instantly, *there* you do not believe in the power of your own mind; therefore, you only know your limitations.'

'But these things here, they manifest instantly? Over *there* that would not be so?'

'Here there is no notion of time, time does not exist in any dimension, but you have the belief that it does, so it is so.' I felt my brain beginning to turn into a pretzel, 'It is this illusion of time that you are governed by, what possible use can it serve when you are all so convinced there is never enough of it?'

I didn't respond.

'Can you imagine what would happen if all humans could manifest instantaneously? You're all so focused on the things you don't want, those are exactly the things that would show up for you.' the voice continued, 'You'd ruin your own lives by doing this, you need to focus so much on the positive that that's all will show up for you. Therefore, there is a "buffer period", if you will, on earth so that in order to manifest things into your reality, you have to give them a considerable amount of attention.'

'So, I could in theory manifest something that I don't want, if I think too long about it?'

'Yes, the universe does not know the difference between what you do or do not want, it only responds to that which you focus on.' I felt a strong desire to lay down.

It's been four weeks since then. Four weeks I have been here in this 'other world', experiencing all the wonderful things I can manifest, the places I can visit.

I wonder how long before I wake up, *will I ever wake up?* I'm not quite dead, but I'm not living either. I watch myself each day in a vegetative state, confined to my bed, plugged in and wired up to some machine. Many people come to visit me, mum and dad barely leave my side. *Even dad's snoring isn't enough to wake me.*

Most days I drift off, visiting all my favourite places. Today I sat down in the field not far from my house. It was a sunny, summers afternoon and nobody was around. I could feel the warmth on my skin, the smell of the long grass, the flowers, the sound of the bee's as they buzzed past my face. I was happy, content. Within a few minutes I was in a place of total relaxation. My mind, my body, everything, was calm and still. I began to feel this energy rising through my body, pulsating, twisting, buzzing, whooshing. It began at my spine and worked its way up to the crown of my head, reaching every inch of my body. The sensation suddenly became so intense that I wanted to scream, not in pain, but in frustration. I felt I was being, not dragged, but *called* away. I was so relaxed I didn't want to move. I laid down in the grass, ignoring it. I looked up at the sky and noticed how blue it was, how all the colours around me were seemingly much brighter. I noticed that all my senses had been heightened – everything smelled, sounded, and felt different, more…*alive*. I was curious to know how far I could travel from my body, so I explored a bit further each time before returning to watch over my parents and my empty shell of a body. I realised this is what it feels like to have an endless day, to require nothing, no food, no water, no sleep. I'm beginning to get a little tired of it. I'm restless, and with each day that passes I feel a call from somewhere in the back of my mind or in the distance. A call to walk away, but I don't want to die, I want to wake up. *I am desperate to wake up.*

Could I die here if I'm only half dead? What would happen if I just threw myself off a cliff? Would it be like a video game and I'd restart back at the last checkpoint? I decide I don't want to find out, so I turn my focus to something else. I walk through the hospital, wandering the halls, watching the doctors and nurses and visitors pass by. I stop in front of one and they walked straight through me. I'm invisible to everyone, to my mum and my dad, to my friends. Nobody can see me, but I can see them. *I am stuck here in this in-between, alone, and I don't know how to wake up.*

'WAKE UP! WAKE UP! WAKE UP!' I scream and shout, but nothing happens. I go back to my room and sit down on the floor; sobs start to come uncontrollably from me. I am trapped here, with no one to talk to. *I just want my life back.* I close my eyes and wish for sleep.

Each day is a drag, and I've come to the sudden realisation that there is no satisfaction here, no joy to be had when I do not require anything to survive. Anything I think of, I can have. *Where is the challenge in that?* Anything I can think of, *except waking up.*

I hear that voice again, this time, I call out to it, 'Hello? Can you help me, please?' I feel that whooshing sensation again in my body, a feeling of love washes over me.

'Hello dear one,' the voices replies.

'Please, I want to wake up, I don't want to die.'

'Then you must stop fighting, resistance is futile. If you want to live, you must surrender.'

'Surrender to what?'

'Surrender to the life force that exists all around you. You must realise that you are infinite, that there is no such thing as death. Only that which is the opposite of love can end, and anything that is not love is an illusion. *You cannot die.*'

'Your very essence is love, there is no separation between you and the source that created you, therefore, you are infinite.'

'But, my family, I can't leave them!'

'The question is not, do you want to die, but, do you want to live?'

'Yes! Yes, I want to live.'

'But you acted in a way that would suggest otherwise...'

Shame fills my being; I know exactly what this voice is going to say. I can't speak, 'You drove recklessly, you had no regard for leaving your family then?'

'I was wrong.'

'You tried to end your life.'

'I was wrong. Please, tell me how I can fix this?'

'It is when you forget who you are that you find yourself. It is when you forgive yourself that you are forgiven. It is when you die that you awaken to eternal life.'

'But I don't want to die!'

'As you have said many times now.'

The voice continues,

'Would you have chosen to live if you had not experienced death?'

The question stuns me for a moment, 'No.'

'Many people do not choose to live; they wait to die.'

Tears stream from my face, 'I was foolish and selfish, and I wanted my life to be over.'

'Your life is over, *the life you knew.'* the voice explains,

'When you wake up you will not be the same person you were before, it would be impossible.'

'*When* I wake up?'

'You chose to live, did you not?'

I sink to my knees, crying with happiness. 'I am so grateful, thank you, *thank you!*

'Do not thank me, *you* are the one who made the choice, none can make it for you.'

'The gift of life is yours to experience, but many consider it to be a curse not a blessing.'

'It is indeed a blessing, and I will no longer see myself as a victim of circumstance.' I stand up tall and begin to feel air filling my lungs, 'I understand I have the potential to create the life I desire, I need only ask and allow it to show up in my life!'

The voice did not speak again, but a strong ringing resounded in my ears. Growing higher and higher in pitch, until barely audible.

I begin to feel extremely tired, exhausted. So

much so, that I can barely move. I want to lie down, to sleep but I'm not sure how. A soft breeze blows away the ground beneath my feet, carrying it away like dust. The walls of my room disappear the same way, revealing bright, golden light streaming towards me from every angle. I am enclosed in a blanket of golden sunlight, warming my skin. The light grows so brightly that I am unable to keep my eyes open and they flutter shut. I just want to sleep and finally I do...

'Sweetheart?' a hand brushes my cheek, *mum.*

'She's awake! Quick, tell the nurse she's out of the coma!' I hear the sweet sound of two familiar voices as I awake to life once more...

8

FELIX FIELD

SUNLIGHT, ITS GOLDEN BEAMS SHINE down upon me, turning the inside of my eyelids pink whilst my eyes softly shut. I lay on my back, arms resting on my stomach, the luscious field grass holding me close with its scattered wild daisies tickling at my skin. My nose wrinkles as I stifle a sneeze, *hay-fever*. My lips curl upwards at their edges as a warm breeze rushes over my body, Mother Nature hugs me in every direction. I smooth down the skirt of my summer dress as the breeze ruffles it playfully, it's white with dozens of blue Forget-Me-Nots all over it - a little grass stained now.

My eyes open to a beautiful array of wispy clouds in the sky, their shapes and patterns creating stories in my mind. I like to bring the twins, Felix and Dotty here to cloud watch with me sometimes.

You can never keep Felix still, he's usually running around like a mad thing, but Dotty is very much like me, she'll lay beside me for hours looking up at the big, blue sky and we'll point and giggle at the funny shapes and make up stories about the characters in the clouds. Sometimes we bring a picnic that Mother has made for us, we fill the picnic basket with half a dozen jam sandwiches and biscuits. I let Dotty eat a few on the way as we walk to our field – or, as we've so rightly named it, Felix Field on account of Felix being the one who discovered it. He was three years old and one day we couldn't find him anywhere, we were all frantically looking for him. Dotty insisted I went with her as she led me away from the house, I protested and told her we didn't have time to play. I remember her little face as her eyes welled up in frustration and her bottom lip protruded about an inch from the other,

'Okay little one,' I said, 'where are you taking me?' and we raced along heading straight through overgrown bushes until we reached the other side. My astonishment when, not only had we arrived at the most heavenly of all places, but that we found Felix, my little brother sat down in the middle of it making daisy chains.

To this day I'm not sure how Dotty knew he'd be there, perhaps it's that telepathic twin thing that I've read about before. The twins are five now and we visit Felix Field almost every day, well, *we did.* For a while now Mother has made them stay home, said that after school they can't go out and play like we used to, said they're not even allowed to go in my room anymore.

Mother's not been herself since the accident. Back in the winter, the lake nearby had completely frozen over. I've always loved skating across it, I'm quite good, but suddenly the ice cracked beneath my feet and I fell in, hitting my head on the way down. The thing is, *I can't swim.*

It's very quiet here without the twins, no Felix running around pretending he's a lion or a bear or whatever his mind comes up with next. No Dotty and I laughing as we take turns brushing each other's hair, sometimes I'll practice my French plait on her mousey brown locks, but I've never been much good at those.

A whooshing sensation fills my head as I sit upright. The smell of strawberry jam fills my nose as I take out a sandwich from my pocket. Two Red Admiral butterflies dance together above my head, so light, so free. It's not fair for the twins to miss this. This is our place after all, our little haven free from the big bad world where the twins don't get picked on at school for having holes in their shoes.

I stay for a little while longer then make my way back to the house leaving my fourteen-year-old indent in the grass. Our rickety old gate creaks and swings in the breeze as I walk up the garden path. Our garden is filled with flowers all in bloom. Pretty pink peonies and vibrant fuchsias sit in various pots, clematis climbs up every trellis and Dotty's favourite flower of all creeps through the cracks in the paving stones, *dandelions.*

Our front door is open ajar as I approach it, strange. I'm quick to remove my shoes before entering, Mother hates mud walked into the carpets. Our home is a modest three bedroom, although the twin's room is barely big enough for one of them let alone two. It appears no one is home, which makes me wonder where they all are. Mother doesn't ever take the twins out by herself, says she can't handle two of the little terrors. They're no trouble for me, probably because we have lots of fun and I let them get away with all sorts. It's been hard for Mother since Father went off to war. The twins don't seem to remember much of him, Mother says he'll be back. *That was years ago.*

I miss father, how he'd read to me before bed, using all sorts of funny voices. How he used to make mother laugh. *I've not heard her laugh since.* Sometimes I think I see him, glimpses of him walking through the halls of the house. I dream of him too, he's always smiling, happy to see me. He asks me to take his hand and go with him, that there's nothing to be frightened of, I tell him I don't want to go, that I must stay here with the twins, *with mother.* They need me. Although, sometimes it doesn't feel like a dream, sometimes I feel as though I don't sleep at all, not anymore.

Most nights I read or pace my room. One night I got so fed up I crept downstairs and ran to Felix Field. The sky was so clear, the moon was out and bigger than I'd ever seen it and all the stars in the galaxy were shining brilliantly! I didn't want to go back, back to the house where I couldn't sleep. I waited until morning and drifted back in, floated up the stairs and collapsed on my bed. Sometimes I feel so drained if I'm away from the house too long, the field is about as far as I feel I can make.

In my room, I hear the faintest of noises like mice whispering. I creep up to the door slowly and push it slightly. There, sat on the floor, are the twins. I startle them with my presence, and they jump up quick, scared it's mother,

'What are you two monkeys' doing in here?' I ask, kissing the top of Dotty's head. She giggles up at me and hands me a piece of paper. It's a drawing she's made of herself, Felix and me. It's so lovely it makes my eyes well up. In the picture, the three of us are sat in Felix Field eating red splodges – *I think they're jam sandwiches.* I notice in the drawing there is a white ring above my head. *It's a halo.*

'Dotty what is this for?'

'Because you're an angel Alice,' she smiles. Felix takes me by the hand and leads me toward mothers' room. I peak through the gap in the door, she is lying down asleep on her bed. Felix opens his mouth and pats his tummy, telling me he's hungry. *Felix doesn't speak.* Not because he's not able to, but one day he just stopped. Ever since my accident, Felix hasn't spoken a word. It's probably a good thing, as Dotty talks enough for the whole of England sometimes.

The three of us traipse downstairs in search of some bread and jam. It's about 7 o'clock before mother comes down to join us, her hair matted, and lips chapped. Felix rushes to her side and pulls at her,

'Not now Felix!' Mother shouts, pouring herself a glass of water. Dotty takes Felix by the hand and the two scurry off back to their room.

'What is the matter Mother?' I ask, she only glances my way. She tips two pills into her mouth and I place a hand on hers to prevent the third from going any further. She whips her hand away and takes a step back as if I've hurt her somehow. The third pill goes down with a mighty gulp, slamming the glass on the kitchen counter.

'Dotty, Felix,' her voice weak and strained, 'darlings come here.'

They must have been sat at the top of the stairs

because they come crashing down like boulders, Felix nearly tripping on his shoelaces along the way.

'Come here you two,' Mother's voice gentler now, soothing, 'Mummy's sorry for shouting Felix,' she places a kiss on each of their heads and the three of them share a loving embrace. I step forward myself. Mother's so frail, and the twins are such saplings that I can easily wrap my arms around all of them. Dotty giggles which sets us all off laughing, a melodious noise escapes from Mother, she can't stop. Her laughter soon turns to tears though, I'm not sure if she is happy or sad. Or both.

'Oh, my angels, I love you all so very much.'

'We love you too Mummy,' Dotty squeaks.

Felix wipes away mothers tears and pecks her on the nose. We stand together for a while, the four of us, *our little family.*

The next morning, I hear commotion downstairs, the twins are shrieking and jumping with excitement. I see mother in her Sunday dress, *expect it's Saturday.* She looks happy. She's delicately placing something in a basket, our picnic basket. I step closer to find out what's inside - *jam sandwiches!*

'Mother where are we going?' I'm happy and confused at the same time, 'You've made sandwiches?' are we going where I think we're going? Together? As a family?

'Come on darlings, off to Felix Field we go!' The twins bound on hand in hand out of the garden, mother carrying the basket. The four of us push through the bushes and pop out the other side. It's as glorious as ever, sun beaming down upon the lush green grass. We play for a while and then we sit, we eat, we laugh some more. I see Mother's eyes glittering, welling up. She reaches a hand into the basket, pulling something else out, something I hadn't noticed before. *A little wooden box.*

'Darlings I think it's time we let her go.'

Let who go? she holds the box delicately to her chest.

'Who Mummy?' says Dotty.

'Your sister.'

No. Tears cascade from my eyes, plummeting down my dress. It can't be. I'm not...*am I?*

'Will she be in heaven Mummy?' Dotty asks. 'With Daddy?'

I don't understand.

'Yes, my sweet, with Daddy.'

No! I shout but they don't even look. *They can't hear me!*

I watch as they stand together, the three of them. Mother carefully opens the box. Soft, grey dust escapes carried off by a gust of wind.

'Goodbye Alice,' they say in unison, 'we love you.' *But I don't want to leave you!* I gasp, feeling as light as air, a calming sensation washing over me. I try to resist it. *I really, really try,* but suddenly I realise, *I don't want to.* I feel as if part of me has been carried away in the breeze. I feel odd, I feel...*free.*

There is a man stood beside me, his arms find me and hold me close. This man is loving and kind, he brushes some hair from my face,

'Hi chicken,' all fear, all sadness fades away and is replaced by a soft, gentle buzzing feeling that surrounds my whole body.

I know the man's voice, his soothing tone, *his presence,* it's my Daddy.

'It's all going to be okay.' he takes my hand and this time I don't resist; I go happily with him. We walk together, smiling as we watch the twins laugh and frolic with Mother. I know I can go now; *they don't need me anymore.*

Father and I walk on towards the sun, smiling. I know wherever I'm headed, there will always be a part of me here, with them, *in Felix Field.*

9

BROUGHT TO LIFE

HE DOESN'T REMEMBER, BUT I DO. *I remember everything.* They say memory is a gift, I disagree. In this instance, memory is a curse, something that won't let me go for as long as I exist.

I wish to forget him altogether at times, to let him

get on with it, *but I can't.*

Every human gets assigned an angel, to watch over them, to protect them. We can't intervene – *believe me, I'd love to*, but we can step in at times when needed. No, we don't have wings, and no, we can't fly. Unfortunately for me, I got lumbered with *him.*

He looks different in every lifetime of course, different body, different hair, everything changes. Except the eyes, *the eyes always stay the same.* The eyes being the window to the soul, their true self, which never changes. He was sixteen when I was sent to him, perhaps that's why he annoyed me so much – *I know way too much about teenage boys than I ought to know.* How he survived without me up until then I have *no* idea.

I've always wondered why he didn't already have an angel, had they forgotten about him? Adjusting to my new job was proving much too difficult at first. Everybody else was lovingly watching over their *assignments* like proud parents. I on the other hand, was busy trying to figure out what it was about mine that annoyed me so much. I even considered the possibility there was something wrong with me, that maybe I'd been assigned to the wrong person. I was assured, *much to my disappointment,* this was not the case.

I couldn't put my finger on it, but there was something about him which made me uneasy - *and that annoyed me more than anything.* By the time he was thirty, I had stepped in so many times to save his life - the amount of times that man has nearly electrocuted himself, *even today*, is terrifying. In which case of course, I'd just switch off all his power - *I quite enjoyed that.*

Then there's the numerous occasions where he's practically choking to death on his own vomit. I'd roll my eyes in frustration, wondering why he always got himself in such a state. Then I'd realise he would probably die if I didn't do anything. Needless to say, *no gold stars for this angel.*

There was one night, during that first lifetime

with him, when I saw something in his eyes that I'd never seen before, *fear.* He's not easily phased by life and if anything was bothering him nobody on earth would ever know about it. *But I wasn't somebody on earth.* I could tell there was something on his mind, he was unsettled and anxious. He walked home from work in the rain, collapsed on the bathroom floor, and for the first time, I saw him cry. I wasn't sure how to react, I felt quite uncomfortable, seeing him that way. In that moment I decided I no longer disliked him; I had finally seen the real him.

Up until that point he'd been busy numbing out the world. Every poor decision he made, every person he shut out, it was because deep down inside, despite everything, he was afraid of love. He was afraid of *losing* love. That's why I never saw him get close enough to anybody to love them. He'd go on dates of course, but he knew inside it was going nowhere, he wouldn't allow it. It's a good theory I guess, *you can't lose love if you never risk loving anyone.* I thought how lonely it must be in his heart, never letting anyone in.

I sat beside him that night on the floor, I wanted to understand him. *I wanted to help him.* After crawling into bed and finally falling asleep, he woke not long after in a cold sweat. I hadn't left his side all night, and although he couldn't see me, I watched as terror consumed him. Bolted upright in his bed, eyes wide with fear. He was looking directly behind me. When I turned to see what was there, in the corner of that room, I wanted to hide. *A black mass hovered.* I was seeing what he was seeing that black shadow was all his fears, worries, and pain. With my hand over his heart I matched his heartbeat to my own, slow and steady. As he fell back to sleep, I did something I'd never done before, I leaned over him and placed a kiss on his forehead.

As angels, we have one major rule, no matter how much we care for our assigned souls, we must never, *ever* fall in love with them. This is because angels aren't meant to live on earth. If an angel stays too long on earth, they get sick. Each time we visit earth we get a little weaker — though this has a lot to do with human interaction and various...*activities.* Many angels in the past have indeed fallen, meaning they got a taste of life on earth and didn't want to leave. Fallen angels lose their abilities, they are no longer fit for purpose. They become - well, I'll get to that...

As for falling in love, *well I knew that was never going to happen.*

According to the angel handbook — *I'm kidding, there isn't one,* another rule you must never, ever break under any circumstances, is let your assignment see you, the real you. I don't know exactly why this is, unless some crazy imprinting thing goes on — *or we're all too ridiculously beautiful to be seen.* To get around this however, we can visit earth in the form of a human body.

I can't explain the feeling of meeting him properly for the first time. I wanted so desperately for him to know me, *to see me.* It was no longer enough that I could watch him in secret, to know the side of him no one else sees, I wanted to interact with him, I wanted to get to know him in the same way everyone else got to. *I wanted to know what it felt like to look into his eyes and see him staring back.* I wanted it so badly I could scream. I thought about it, I thought about it so many times, just showing up in his life, right there and then, but I couldn't do it. I waited until that life was over, until he had lived it all.

As I watched over him for the rest of his days, I thought about how I would appear to him in his next life, how I would dress, how I would walk, my hair colour, the sound of my voice. I didn't know what I was expecting or how long our meeting would be, all I knew is that it had to happen, *and I would wait patiently for that day to arrive.*

I have been there since he first opened his eyes, when he said his first word, his first crush, his first grey hair. *His last breath.* I have watched him make the best and worst choices, I've watched him find and lose love, I've watched him get married and raise his own family, and I've watched him sink into a dark depression praying it would all go away. I could tell you the songs he sings in the shower, or the way he loses himself as he contemplates the very nature of his existence, I could tell you everything about him, and now I can tell you how he looked at me on that very first meeting.

It was a hot summers day in July, he was twenty-four. I didn't plan the date, although I knew his routine, I also knew how he would get bored and occasionally do something completely different. *This was one of those days.* Usually, he'd wake up, take a shower, and grab a coffee before going to work. I knew acquiring a physical vessel would prevent me from sensing where he was, which was worrying, but I knew he'd be out of his apartment for a while and I needed a safe place to get used to my new body. *I also needed to figure out how quickly I could leave it.*

In front of the mirror, stood a petite, casually dressed female, with long brown hair and two blue eyes staring back at me. *My eyes.* I'd spent long enough observing humans to know that no two are the same, that some are taller, shorter, rounder, thinner. I thought very much about being one of those cosmetically proportioned women with the strategically placed curves and the tiny waists, the ones all the men seem to like. Until I realised, *he doesn't.* Whenever someone like that walks by him, he always looks away. I was confused. The ones he does notice, are the ones that smile a lot, who have some sort of earthly charm about them, the ones that are polite and caring, almost as if they were angels themselves. I stood there in front of the mirror, wondering if he'd like me. Then after that, I threw up.

I was so grateful I was alone. I didn't realise how different the energy would feel being in a physical body, how the air would feel so stuffy. I felt like I was underwater and there was this indescribably annoying ringing in my ears. I prayed he wouldn't come home. After what felt like an eternity - *which I'd know all about,* the room finally stopped moving and I was able to walk in a straight line. I didn't know where he was, but I thought about where he might be.

Walking down the street felt impossible, everything was so loud and bright, people were moving too fast, cars were everywhere, the fumes choking my lungs. My senses were so heightened that my vision was impaired, and I was seemingly staring through a kaleidoscope - *all the while, trying desperately to hold on to my stomach.* I had never been drunk, but I imagined that's partly what it felt like. It wasn't this so much that concerned me, but the fact people were staring, *and they were staring at me.* I almost thought I wouldn't make it to the coffee shop, but there I was at the door, walking inside.

He wasn't there. He was nowhere to be seen. Part of me was relieved, I realised I'd made a huge mistake and I didn't want to spend another minute in that skin suit. I was annoyed at myself for wasting so much time thinking about this day when I couldn't even last five minutes, but I forced myself to act somewhat human and sat down at a table. Something resembling mud poured down my throat, it nearly came out of my nose. People looked over as I choked on it and refrained from spitting it back in my cup. *Coffee, they call it.* As I got up to leave someone walked in the door, someone who I was unable to walk past. *It was him.* I couldn't believe it. There he was, there I was. We came face to face, his beautiful brown eyes staring down at me, it was the first time I had noticed the flecks of amber in them.

I didn't speak, I didn't know what to say. He just stared at me, this puzzling look on his face and I knew exactly what he was thinking, 'Do I know you from somewhere?' *Yes, you do.*

I thought about running, it would have been so much easier, but I couldn't seem to drag myself away from him. I could barely breathe; the air was heavy and congested. He asked me to sit with him and we quickly became immersed in conversation. I tried very hard not to bring up anything I already knew about him. I tried my hardest to act like a normal human being, but it was the slight nervousness I caught in his laugh that made me relax.

There was something about the way he looked at

me, how every so often he would wrinkle his brow in confusion and in those moments, I wondered if he knew who I was. What I found most unusual, was how I felt after our first meeting, how watching him suddenly felt so wrong. I didn't want to pretend with him, I didn't want to lie about who I was or where I grew up. The only thing I didn't have to lie about was my name,

'Sera.'

'Sera?' his voice was like music to my ears.

'Seraphina, but just call me Sera.'

'Seraphina, like the angel?'

I smiled, 'Yes.'

Our meetings became more frequent after that. Of course, I never stuck around after, I couldn't get out of that body fast enough. Besides, a few hours on earth now and again never hurt anyone, right?

A few weeks later, I experienced first-hand what kissing felt like. I'm sure kissing anyone else would not have been so extraordinary, but kissing him, *well that was something I'd never grow tired of.* It was the way he ran his hand gently down my cheek, lifting my chin until my eyes met his, reaching about 90% of the way to my lips, lingering there until I couldn't help but go the rest of the way. All of this had made realise what it truly meant to be human, to experience such feelings, sensations and moments that I had been deprived of.

We were always laughing, smiling, fooling around together. I began spending nights with him, just us, alone together for hours upon hours. I never wanted it to end. His every touch was like velvet on my skin; soft and something I couldn't get enough of. We had months this. Months I carried this feeling of joy, happiness and euphoria within me. But in the back of my mind I knew, *I knew it couldn't last forever.*

It was becoming increasingly obvious that my time on earth was the cause of much fatigue I had been experiencing. Eventually I started to feel ill. I hated being away from him physically. I never left him, not really, but he didn't know that. The time I did spend with him got so bad I started having nosebleeds. I tried to hide them from him, I tried to hide it all from him. To see what it did to him, to see how he became the one to lay awake and watch me sleep, it was soul-destroying. Sometimes I didn't even have the strength to move, to go back.

I laid there all night on the bathroom floor, being sick. I woke up in a hospital bed, dizzy and plugged into some machine. I remember overhearing the doctors telling him they didn't understand, they couldn't find a cause.

Weeks went by, he never left my side. I didn't know what was happening to me, I couldn't die, *could I?* Still, I couldn't find the strength to leave, not my body, *but him.* I knew if I left, it would have to be for good. I was selfish for staying as long as I did, I should never have let it go on so long. *I should never have gone in the first place.* I finally found the strength to leave he was asleep on the bed beside me, his arms wrapped gently around me.

I had run out of options, I had to go. I had to leave before it was too late, 'Goodbye my love,' I placed a kiss on his forehead without waking him, 'I'm sorry, please forgive me.'

That's when I discovered what was happening, all that time I'd spent on Earth, it wasn't killing me. All the fatigue and the nosebleeds, it wasn't because I was dying, I was becoming human! *I was becoming one of the fallen.*

As painful as it was, I decided I could only watch him from afar. Appearing as an acquaintance, a work colleague, a friend. *A best friend.* Just so I could know him again, just so I could be a part of his life again. Even that got too much. I was a terrible friend, always running away from him. It was never enough, and it never would be enough. I knew his touch, I knew him in a way I didn't know him before, in a way that watching him all those years could never teach me.

I was sick and tired of watching him with women who had no idea how to love him. Having grown exceptionally bored and tired of my life at that point - *eternity is a very long time,* I began wandering the earth, exploring, for my own amusement. It is not permitted of course, but I did it anyway. He was Will by then, a tall, handsome man with a good heart and a great smile. It was hard, knowing he didn't remember a thing, *knowing I would always be the one to remember.* That is the angels curse, while everyone else grows, evolves, lives, we watch, protect, observe. There's only one way to end the cycle, but it comes at a cost.

I sat by the water. I liked it there, it soothed me, the soft shh-ing of the sea as it swayed in and out, in and out. I looked at the passers-by, how they, like the water, flowed through life. Some like rivers that move gently, some like a babbling brook full of life and sound. *Some like a tsunami that destroy everything in their wake.* Was I water? Did I move like the sea? Or was I trapped in a well, still, stagnant, *not flowing at all.*

I wished to be free. Free like them, like those people who take life for granted, who don't have to be something for someone, who don't have to watch the person they love live without them over and over and over until it slowly drives them mad. The hours passed; my eyes fixed on the horizon. I was so consumed by the sea, that I didn't notice the figure appear a few feet away from me. A man.

'It's beautiful, isn't it?' he too had his eyes fixed on the horizon. There is something about being in the wrong place at the wrong time that always seems to feel like exactly the right place at the right time. Right then, I was exactly in the wrong place, at the wrong time.

'It certainly is beautiful, Will.'

He turned and looked at me, the same way he had all those times before, with those eyes that never changed. Only, this time it was different, this time those eyes saw me, *the real me.* I didn't know what was going to happen next. *Would I evaporate, turn to dust?* He stared, wrinkling his forehead in confusion. *I shouldn't be here; he shouldn't be here.*

'I know you,' he moved towards me, I stepped back, 'you're the one I see in my dreams.'

I laughed, 'Do you use that line on all the girls?'

'I'm serious,' and he was, 'it's you isn't it? *You're* the angel.'

I didn't know how it was possible, how he could have seen me. *Was I not careful enough?*

'Since I was a child, I always had this dream, there was an angel watching over me,' he stood in front of me, 'it's you, isn't it?'

I couldn't lie any longer. I couldn't, *I wouldn't!* It wasn't fair, I was so, so lonely. I told him who I was, How I'd always been there, how we had met before, *many, many times before.* I didn't care anymore, I was so tired of keeping it all in, of holding on to all those memories, I wanted him to know, *I wanted him to remember.* I told him why I could never stay on Earth, why we could never be together, that I would always have to leave him.

'There must be a way,' he said, 'I don't want you to go.'

'The only way for an angel to live on Earth, is if they choose to stay.'

'Then stay,' his words echoed in my mind, over

and over.

'If I stay, then I have to stay forever, I can't go back.'

'Isn't that what you want?' he took my hand, 'To be with me?'

'Will, if I stay, then I die at the end same as you do, I come back again the next time the same as you.'

'Then we never have to be apart.' he didn't understand.

'Will, when we come back, we won't remember any of this. You won't remember me,' I paused, 'I won't remember *you.*'

Even he didn't know what to say for a moment, 'Then we'll find each other.'

'We won't know each other exist.'

'I will, I'll know you're out there somewhere, I'll find you.'

'I can't take that risk.' Risk, that word again. I remembered him when he was a different man, how he pushed everyone away. Had I been doing the same thing? Running from what I wanted most of all, the love I wanted most of all. *The man I wanted most of all.* I wanted so much to believe it, that I wouldn't have to leave him again, but I knew that eventually I would lose him anyway. It was even harder to go back then, because although he didn't have any memories of us, some part of him knew who I was, something inside him recognised me.

Life was what I wanted, Will was what I wanted. But could I really live on Earth? With all the noise and the people, could I really survive? What about after it all, when I came back? I wouldn't remember a thing; I wouldn't have any memories. I would think I had always been human; *I would have lost Will and I wouldn't even know it.*

I don't know if he truly believed that somehow, we would find each other again, or whether he just wanted me to stay for as long as possible. I thought about it long and hard, for what seemed like forever, but really, I knew I'd already made the decision the second he'd asked me to stay.

My two-year-old daughter sits playing with my hair, I watch my six-year-old son play with his father in the garden.

'Are you hungry sweetheart?' to which she nods very enthusiastically. I serve lunch to my family, 'Boys, food!'

We sit together, laugh, talk, smile, the sun warm on our backs. We are the happiest of families. My husband sits beside me, our daughter climbing his shoulders whilst our son wolfs down his food. He looks at me the same way he always has, with those same brown eyes. Even now, I know exactly what he's thinking, 'Thank you'.

Smiling, I place a kiss on his cheek. When the time comes, I'll forget. Forget my life as an angel, forget my children, *forget Will.* But I know in my heart someday we'll find each other again. No matter where we are in the world, no matter the circumstances. I know it as strongly as I know my love for him, and if a love like that can bring an angel to life, *what can't it do?*

10

CREATION

A BLISSFUL WAVE WASHED OVER HER body as she danced at the water's edge. The sun cast diamonds upon the surface of her skin, glistening like the ocean in her eyes. Her lips parted as she whistled and played with the sound of her own voice. Melodious and gentle, *like a soft spring breeze.* Flaming curls of auburn hair cascaded down her back, swaying and swishing, a soft tickle against her snow-white skin.

She dipped her toes in the ocean, and as she did so, waves came crashing towards her, threatening her gentle disposition. But she stood tall and strong, feet firmly planted on the earth. Roots grew deep from the soles of her feet, impregnating into the soil, connecting her with Mother Nature's sweet soul. Birds flocked above her head, eager to nest in her hair, knowing every creature born of earth can surely find a home in her heart.

As the sun melted away from her palms, the moon returned once again to take his place. The light of Luna illuminated the infinite night, and every star came out to greet her. It was thought up that the sun and the moon would be distant lovers, only ever catching glimpses of each other, to demonstrate, *love does not require touch to be felt.* As the sun and the moon are proof that love lights up the earth, so too are the seasons' a promise that; after darkness the light will always return.

She looked up at the night sky, it wrapped itself around her like a cosmic blanket and stars shot across her skin. She breathed out from the earth, holding it in her hands. She was pleased with what she saw, the natural beauty contained within. But it was not yet finished.

She inhaled the stars, and as she breathed out life from her lungs, the stars split in two, falling gently to the earth, assuming many shapes and sizes. When they'd forgotten who they were, she'd send more down to remind them. As she watched over each of them closely, counting every hair on their heads, mapping every freckle in her mind, and ensuring every fingerprint was unique - *no matter how many came to play,* she marvelled at her creation, knowing it was the most perfect thing she had ever made.

You may notice her; in the kindness of a stranger, in the laughter of a child, or in the arms of a loved one. But really, you need only look in the mirror to see, *her reflection is right there.*

About the Author

Victoria currently lives in a seaside town in Dorset, England where she grew up. Since a child, she has had an insatiable love of books and always expressed her dream of writing her own one day. Writing has been her escape from the world, creating characters and worlds that she loses herself in. As well as her passion for writing, Victoria is an artist and enjoys anything where her creativity can flourish. Inspired by nature, music, classic literature, art, and life itself, Victoria has an imagination that reaches into other dimensions and hopes her readers will enjoy the journey. She is a freespirit who loves connecting with like-minded souls all over the world and has many pen-pals who she loves writing to. Other interests of hers are yoga, Ayurveda, metaphysics, astrology, spirituality, and meditation.

Victoria is making plans to travel the world to satisfy her wanderlust soul and to experience the beauty this world has to offer. Volunteer work and charitable organisations are close to her heart, and she would one day like to set up her own organisation to help make a difference in the lives of others.

Victoria achieved her BA (Hons) in English Literature & Creative Writing, and wrote her debut novel, whilst working at her local Post Office. Victoria is ambitious and hard-working, and believes anything is possible if you set your mind to it. Victoria creates content for a a range of platforms, including: YouTube, social media, and her website. You can found out more and join her email list at:

www.victoriahope.co.uk

Follow: @setyoursoul.free
YouTube: Victoria Hope

To find out about Victoria's other work, books, and to stay in the loop, visit:

www.victoriahope.co.uk

FOR YOU, THE READER

Before closing this book, I want to thank you for taking the time to read it. Whether you bought a copy or were given a copy - or if you're a family member or friend who was *absolutely* obliged to read it. I want to say that it's more than a book to me, and whether you found something within these pages or not, there is at least one thing I'd like you to walk away with, my gratitude.

The tenth story came at the last minute, when this book was already in the process of being published, but I felt it was missing something, it needed a tenth story. Out of all of them, it was the quickest to write, and as I re-read it I wonder who in fact wrote it because it flowed from my pen straight to the page as if it had been there in my mind all along. I think it's the best way to end this book, because oftentimes we forget how powerful we are, how extraordinary we are, we forget *who* we are.

Ultimately, it doesn't matter how long it takes for you to get to where you want to be, you don't even have to know where exactly that is, you need only to go boldly in that direction. It can be easy to doubt ourselves, our abilities, but we must remember that nothing worth having ever comes easy. We have to make these things happen for ourselves - *you* are the only person standing in your way.

As the character in *Life After Death* discovers,

"It is when you forget who you are that you find yourself. It is when you forgive yourself that you are forgiven. It is when you die that you awaken to eternal life."

When I look at the words on these pages, my own words, when I hold this book in my hands, a book with my name on it, I feel a tremendous sense of pride. I made this book a reality. It doesn't matter what comes of it, which corners of the earth it reaches, how many copies are sold, it will always be in the hands of the right person.

With my humble thanks, I leave you with this book, it is my honour to have you read it.

With love,
Victoria

VICTORIA HOPE